"넌 저 하늘에서 땅에 무엇이 보여? 난 별 무리가 수놓은 하늘을 바라보곤 했는데…" 꼬마 소녀가 묻자, 별은 대답합니다. "음… 네가 보는 것처럼, 셀 수 없는 반짝임!"

"What can be seen on Earth from up there? I would see the sky with a cluster of shimmering stars…" Petite Girl asked Twinkle Star.
"Hmm… Countless twinkles just like you observe!"

초판 1쇄 발행 2025년 4월 2일

글 • 그림 임현아 | 펴낸이 서영주 | 총편집 김동주 | 편집디자인 임현아 |

펴낸곳 레벤북스 | 출판등록 2019년 9월 18일 제2019-000033
주소 서울특별시 강북구 오현로7길 20
취급처 레벤북스보급소 | 통신판매 02)945-2972
전자우편 lebenbooks@paolo.net | www.paolo.kr

이 책의 저작권은 작가 임현아에게 있습니다. 저작권법에 의해 한국 내에서 보호를 받는 저작물이므로 무단 전재와 무단 복제를 금합니다.
정가 15000원 | ISBN 979-11-991509-0-4

First published in hardback in 2025

ISBN 979-11-991509-0-4
Lebenbooks Publishing House
Text and Illustrations copyright © Hyunah Lim 2025

The author/ illustrator asserts the moral right to be identified as the author/ illustrator of the work. All rights reserved. No part of this publication may be reproduced, stored in a retrieval system or transmitted in any form or by any means, electronic, mechanical, recording or otherwise, without the prior permission of Lebenbooks Publishing House 20 Ohyeonro7gil, Gangbukgu, Seoul, 01166, Republic of Korea.

Lebenbooks Publishing House
20 Ohyeonro7gil, Gangbukgu, Seoul, 01166, Republic of Korea.

Visit our website at www.paolo.kr
Contact email lebenbooks@paolo.net

Printed in Republic of Korea
Price US $ 11.35

바람타고 머물러요

Simply Voyaging

WRITTEN AND ILLUSTRATED BY

HYUNAH LIM

글 • 그림 임현아

레벤북스

할머니와 별수국
Grandma & Star Hydrangea

　오월 따사로운 해가 거실 안 깊숙이 들어왔습니다. 할머니는 햇빛 받아 방긋 피어오른 별 수국을 바라봤어요. 연분홍 꽃이 별 모양으로 반짝거리며 오후의 나른함을 깨웠지요. 할머니는 새순에 핀 여린 꽃을 보고 미소 짓습니다. 그리고 햇살이 가득한 꽃잎을 보며 기억 속 여행길을 떠납니다.

The warm May sun penetrates deep into the living room. Grandma gazes at the Star Hydrangea standing upright in the sunlight. The light pink flowers, shimmering like stars, awaken the afternoon's laziness. She smiles at the newly blossomed. Observing the petals illuminated by sunlight, she reminisces about past journeys.

별 내려오다!
Descending Twinkle Star!

바람타고 머물러요

별 무리를 보는 것이 즐거운 꼬마 소녀는 오늘도 문밖으로 나가 까치발을 들었어요. 어둠 내린 하늘에 가까이 다가가 별들을 잘 보기 위해서였죠.

"찾았다!"

꼬마는 늘 그 자리에 있는 작지만, 금빛으로 환히 빛나는 별이 반가웠습니다. 소녀의 밤하늘 여행은 작은 금빛 별을 찾는 데서 시작됐죠.

"이 별 무리는 아기 곰 같고, 저 무리는 여우처럼 보여."

별 보며 꼬마는 누군가와 얘기를 나누는 듯 혼잣말을 하곤 했어요.

그날도 소녀는 밤새 별들을 보다, 어느새 구름 사이 하늘이 붉게 물드는 새벽녘이 됐어요. 산들바람이 살짝 꼬마의 볼에 스쳐 지나갔죠.

"꼬마야 안녕!" 소녀는 금빛 반짝임을 눈앞에 보고 깜짝 놀랐지요.

Petite Girl who enjoyed observing the clusters of stars went outside and stood on her tiptoes. She wanted to get closer to the dark sky to see them better.

"Right here!"

She was delighted to see a small but brightly shimmering gold star still there. Nocturnal explorations would start with finding him.

"This cluster resembles a baby bear, and that one looks like a fox."

She felt as if she was conversing with someone as she spoke to herself, gazing at the stars.

On that day, Petite Girl lost track of the time, observing the clusters of stars throughout the night. The sky painted itself in dawn orange among the clouds. Then Sudden Breeze gently brushed her cheek.

"Hi, Petite Girl!" She was astonished by the bright twinkling light in front of her.

좀 전까지 하늘에 있던 그 금빛 별이 바로 소녀 곁에 있었습니다.

"어떻게 이곳에 왔어?"

소녀는 밤하늘 친구가 온 것이 신기했어요.

"난 네가 왜 혼자 저녁 하늘을 보는지 궁금했거든…"

별이 반짝 미소 지었죠.

"난 깊은 밤하늘에 수놓아진 별 무리를 보곤 했는데, 넌 하늘에서 무엇을 봤어?"

"네가 보는 것처럼, 셀 수 없는 반짝임!"

"땅에도 수많은 반짝임이 보이니?"

별은 환하게 반짝 웃었습니다.

아침 산들바람이 꼬마의 치마를 펄럭 날렸어요. 산 너머 해가 떠오르기 시작했습니다. 금빛 별은 밝아오는 태양에 빛을 잃어갔죠.

Twinkle Star, which had been in the sky, was now beside her.

"How did you come here?"

She was amazed to see the celestial friend descend.

"I was curious why you were alone, gazing up at the night sky…"

He smiled at her.

"I observed the clusters of stars up there. What have you looked at on Earth?"

"Countless twinkles just like you observe!"

"Are there numerous lights visible on Earth?"

Twinkle Star responded with a beaming smile.

At that moment, the morning breeze made her skirt flutter. As the sun rose over the mountain, Twinkle Star's brightness faded beneath its glare.

"어쩌지? 돌아가기엔 너무 늦어버렸어."

"그럼, 우리 함께 있을 안전한 곳을 찾아보자."

하늘에는 노오란빛이 사라지고 해가 눈부시게 빛났습니다. 소녀와 별은 조바심이 났어요.

"여기는 어떨까? 좁지만 깊어서 우리를 쉽게 찾지 못할 거야."

"Oh no, what should we do? It's too late for you to return."

"Then, why don't we find a safe haven?"

The sun's yellow glare vanished, and it was shining. She and her friend fretted.

"How about staying here? It's narrow and deep so that we can't be found easily."

동굴을 발견한 소녀는 별과 함께 온종일 지낼 수 있어 신이 났습니다. 꼬마는 배낭을 메고 집과 동굴을 오갔죠. 큰 배낭에는 동굴에 혼자 있는 친구에게 줄 초콜릿, 우유, 체스 놀이판과 여러 가지가 가득 담겨 있었어요. 별은 꼬마의 이야기에 귀 기울여 주고, 하늘 얘기도 재밌게 해주었지요. 날마다 꼬마의 발걸음은 가벼웠습니다.

She was delighted to spend the entire day with Twinkle Star. She traveled back and forth with a large backpack, packing chocolates, milk, a chess board, and other items her friend in the cave alone would enjoy. He always listened attentively to her and spoke of the marvelous world he came from with delight. The hassles of her daily journey were more happy than troubled her.

* * *

꼬마가 별을 만난 지 사흘째 되는 날, 엄마는 냉장고 안 병에 남은 우유가 평소보다 적은 게 의아했어요. 소녀가 좋아해서 늘 넉넉히 넣어두는 초콜릿이 든 서랍이 텅 비어 있는 것도 이상했죠. 혼자 방에서 노는 일이 많던 소녀는 종일 밖에 나갔다 저물녘 돌아오곤 했어요. 엄마는 평소와 다른 딸이 걱정됐지만, 밝게 웃고 행복한 꼬마 모습에 한편으로는 안심했습니다.

On the third day after their encounter, Mom was bewildered by the unusually low amount of bottled milk left in the refrigerator. The drawer where she kept extra chocolates for her daughter's occasional cravings was also empty. Furthermore, her young daughter, who typically spent time alone in her room, did not return until sunset after being out all day. She was deeply concerned, however, she felt relieved upon seeing her daughter appear happier.

소녀는 그날도 아침부터 커다란 배낭에 이것저것 담아 별이 있는 동굴로 갔습니다. 그런데 어두운 표정의 별을 보자 걱정되어 물었어요.

"별아, 무슨 일 있어?"

별은 아무 일도 없다고 했지만, 꼬마는 하늘에서 별이 친구들과 지내던 날이 그리워서일지 생각했지요.

Petite Girl returned to the cave that morning with her backpack filled with lots of stuff. Seeing Twinkle Star look downcast, she asked.

"Why do you look so sad?"

He remained silent, yet she speculated that his sorrow might stem from missing his celestial companions.

사실 동굴이 비좁아 별은 자유로이 움직이기조차 어려웠습니다. 게다가 어두운 곳에서 더욱 밝게 빛나는 별에게는 깊은 동굴은 안전하지 않았죠. 별은 반짝임을 가진 자신이 사람들의 눈에 띨까, 걱정하는 소녀를 편안하게 해주고 싶었습니다.

"우리 다른 곳을 찾아볼까?"
소녀는 새로운 곳이 친구에게 활기를 줄까 해서 물었어요. 별은 고개를 끄덕였고, 둘은 행복한 곳을 찾는 여행길에 나섰습니다. 그날따라 가방 속에 넉넉히 딸기 웨하스를 넣어온 건 참 잘한 일이었어요.

Indeed, the cave they discovered was too cramped to move around freely. Moreover, it might not have been secure enough for him since the starlight shone brighter within the dark cave. Twinkle Star wished to reassure Petite Girl, who was concerned about others noticing his glow.

"How about finding a new place to stay together?"
She suggested, hoping to refresh his spirit. He was content, and they jumped off a journey to find a safe haven. Packing additional strawberry wafers in her backpack proved to be a wise choice that day.

길 위의 부엉이
Wise Owl on the Road

　'별과 함께 걷던 길에는 흥미로운 모험이 기다리고 있었지. 먹고 마시는 것부터 잠자리를 찾는 건 쉽지 않았지만, 가는 곳곳 새로운 만남이 우리를 반겼어.' 할머니가 화분에 물 주며 기억을 떠올립니다.

　'아침 해가 뜨면 산들바람 따라 우리는 미지의 곳으로 향했어.'

　'Many exciting adventures awaited us along the paths that Twinkle Star and I walked. From eating and drinking to finding a place to sleep, each day was challenging. Yet new encounters greeted us at every turn.' Grandma reminisces her past journey, watering in the potted flowers.

　'Every day, as the sun rose, the morning breeze would guide us to places unknown.'

*　　　*　　　*

꼬마 소녀는 산길로 걸어갔습니다. 숲에서 별과 즐겁게 지낼만한 곳을 찾을 것만 같았어요.

"별아, 아카시아 꽃향기 나지 않니?"

"와, 향이 참 좋다!"

둘은 향기에 이끌려 아카시아가 송이송이 달린 꽃길 따라 가볍게 걸었어요. 벌들이 꽃에 다가가 윙윙 소리 내며 꿀을 따고 있었죠. 그 부지런한 움직임에 사로잡혀 소녀는 쏘일까 하는 두려움도 없이, 가까이서 바라보고 있었습니다.

Petite Girl ventured to the paths leading the forest. She hoped to find a safe haven where they could joyfully spend their time.

"My dear, can you smell the fragrance of Acacia blossoms?"

"Wow, such a pleasant aroma!"

They strolled pleasantly along with clustered Acacia blossoms, inhaling the scents. Bees darted and settled on the flowers to gather nectar, buzzing a constant hum. She watched their industrious efforts intently, unafraid of being stung.

"꼬마들 안녕!"

어디선가 낯선 소리가 들렸어요. 소녀는 깜짝 놀라 얼른 별을 가슴에 안았죠.

"소녀야 안녕!"

꼬마는 소리가 나는 쪽을 향해 두리번거렸지만, 벌들과 아카시아 꽃들만이 있었어요.

"아, 부엉이 할머니였군요! 안녕하세요."

소녀가 올려다본 높은 나뭇가지에 눈을 껌벅껌벅하며 부리가 뾰족한 부엉이가 앉아 있었습니다.

"Hi, you guys!"

A stranger's voice startled her, and she clutched Twinkle Star tightly to her chest.

"Hello, Petite Girl!"

She looked around cautiously, seeing nothing but bees and flowers.

"Ah, it's you! Good morning, Ms. Owl."

Petite Girl finally spotted an old owl with a long beak perched high on a branch, slowly blinking her eyes.

"네 안에 소중한 것이 있구나!" .

부엉이는 낮은 나뭇가지에 내려앉으며 소녀에게 말을 걸었습니다. 소녀는 대답 없이 별을 더욱더 꼬옥 끌어안았죠.

"이 숲에 처음 온 것 같구나."

"할머니는 이곳을 잘 아시나요?"

"응, 난 오랫동안 이 산에서 살고 있단다. 근데 어떻게 여기로 오게 됐니?"

머뭇머뭇하며 주위를 둘러보던 소녀는, 다정하게 말하는 부엉이가 편해져서 조심스레 말문을 열었습니다.

"할머니, 제 안에 무언가 있는 게 보이세요?"

"흠... 얼핏 어떤 빛을 본 것도 같은데."

"네, 맞아요. 별이에요."

"There is something precious inside you!"

Engaging in conversation, Wise Owl perched on the lower branch nearby. Without uttering a word, Petite Girl clutched her friend even more tightly.

"It may be your first time visiting here."

"Are you familiar with this forest?"

"Yes, I have lived here for many years. What brought you two to this place?"

Petite Girl hesitated to speak, but Wise Owl's warm words encouraged her to open up.

"Can't you see the thing inside me?"

"Hmm… at first glance I might see a light."

"Exactly, Twinkle Star."

"그래? 근데 별은 하늘에 있는 거 아니니?"

"네, 그렇죠. 별이 저에게 온 건 놀라운 일이에요. 우린 같이 지낼 안전한 곳을 찾고 있어요."

"안전한 곳이라… 근데 네 친구는 너와 함께 땅에 머물고 싶은 거니?"

"친구도 저와 함께 지낼 곳을 찾자고 했어요."

"Really? But shouldn't a star be in the sky?"

"Right. It's amazing his coming down to see me. We're looking for a safe haven to stay together."

"A safe haven… By the way, does your friend wish to stay here with you?"

"He said to search for it with me."

"이 숲은 너희가 다니기에 조금 위험하지만, 지내기에 좋은 곳이 많이 있단다."

지혜로운 부엉이는 소녀와 별이 안전하게 여행할 수 있도록 숲속 삶에 대해 자세히 알려 주었어요. 꼬마는 부엉이 할머니를 통해 숲이 얼마나 아름다운 곳인지, 새로운 곳에서 모험을 기대하게 됐죠. 그제야 안심이 된 소녀는 별을 가슴에서 놓아주었습니다.

"In this forest, there are numerous locations you could explore, although it's somewhat perilous for you both to roam."

Wise Owl provided them with guidance on how to safely navigate the forest in detail. Listening to her advice, Petite Girl eagerly anticipated witnessing the beauty of the forest and encountering new adventures. Petite Girl was relieved and finally released Twinkle Star from her chest.

"다른 세계에 사는 너희가 함께 지내는 것이 쉽지는 않겠지만, 둘이 함께하기에 낯선 여행에서 서로에게 의지가 될 거야. 때때로 너희가 어려움에 처하면, 어디선가 불어오는 산들바람이 너희에게 새 힘을 줄 거란다!"

지혜로운 부엉이 할머니는 별과 함께 떠나는 꼬마가 멀리 사라질 때까지 손을 흔들어 주었습니다.

"It will be a new adventure for both of you from different worlds. You will rely on each other as you traverse unfamiliar paths. Occasionally, when situations become difficult, a helping breeze will arise from somewhere to aid you!"

Wise Owl waved to them until she vanished into the distance with her companion.

* * *

만물이 보금자리로 되돌아가는 시간이 됐습니다. 한낮에 별이 숨어야 하는 걱정을 하지 않아도 되는 저녁입니다. 별은 소녀가 부엉이 할머니를 만난 후 편안해진 것만으로도 기뻤어요. 소녀는 배낭 안에 가져온 해먹을 나뭇가지에 걸어 잠자리를 만들고, 포옥 들어가 잠이 들었습니다.

아침이 되고 눈을 비비며 잠에서 깬 꼬마는 두 팔 벌려 하늘 친구를 맞았어요.

"친구야 잘 잤니?"

소녀가 밤새 꿈꾸는 동안, 별은 하늘로 올라가서 밝은 빛을 비추어 잠자리를 지켜주었습니다. 그러나 꼬마는 밤사이 일어난 일을 알지 못했지요.

It was time to settle down and return to the place of origin. As the evening shadows deepened, they no longer needed to worry about hiding from the sun. Twinkle Star was pleased that Petite Girl's spirits had lifted after her encounter with Wise Owl. She strung up the hammock she had packed in her backpack between two trees. And she drifted off to sleep within its cozy embrace.

The following morning, Petite Girl greeted her celestial friend with open arms, rubbing her eyes.

"Did you have a restful night?"

Twinkle Star had risen high and kept vigil throughout the night, casting a gentle glow over her as she dreamt. However, she remained unaware of his watchful presence.

느릿느릿 거북이
Slowly, Amiable Turtle

별은 반짝임이 흐릿해졌고 소녀의 눈망울은 아침햇살을 받아 반짝 빛났습니다. 새들의 지저귐과 쉴 새 없이 재잘거리는 소녀 음성이 바람 타고 숲 속으로 퍼져갔습니다.

"오늘은 어디로 갈까?" "저쪽에서 물소리가 나."
소녀와 별은 물소리에 이끌려 옹달샘이 졸졸졸 흐르는 곳으로 향했어요. 꼬마는 두 손 가득 샘물을 떠서 마시고는 별에게도 물을 주었어요. 숲에서 아침은 맑고 시원했습니다.

Twinkle Star's brightness had faded, and the morning sunlight made Petite Girl's eyes shimmer. The chirping of birds and her delightful chattering voice spreaded through the forest on the breeze.

"Where should we go today?" "Listen to that murmuring water."
She and Twinkle Star made their way to the spring where the water rippled gently. After scooping up and drinking two handfuls of water, she handed some to her friend. The morning forest was sunny and fresh.

옹달샘 주위로 조약돌들이 작은 물줄기를 품고 있었지요.

"우리 저 샘물이 어디로 가는지 볼까?"

꼬마는 별에게 손짓하고는 치맛자락을 들고 얕은 물줄기를 찾아 내려갔습니다. 햇살 아래 오리 떼가 날개를 퍼덕이며 노닐고 있는 개울로 시냇물이 흘러 들어가고 있었어요. 소녀는 신발을 벗어들었죠. 발가락 사이로 밀려 들어오는 바닥의 모래 느낌이 좋았습니다. 물을 휘젓고 별에게 장난치며 물을 뿌리고 놀았지요.

Pebbles were sunk in a small stream of water around the spring.

"Why don't we follow the stream?"

Pointing ahead, she strolled along shallow streams, lifting the hem of her skirt. A flock of ducks basked in the sun, leisurely flapping their wings on the water. She removed her shoes, gently feeling the sand beneath her feet. She spent time swirling her hand in the water and playfully splashing it towards Twinkle Star.

한참을 물에서 놀다가, 소녀는 멀리 거북이 두 마리가 평화로이 가는 것을 보았습니다.

"별아, 저 거북이들을 따라가 보자!"

소녀는 물에서 급히 나오려다, 조약돌을 헛디뎌 그만 개울물에 풍덩 빠졌어요.

"앗 차가워. 내 원피스! 엄마가 새로 사주신 건데…"

"저런! 추워서 어쩌지…"

별은 물에 흠뻑 젖은 꼬마를 보고 어쩔 줄 몰랐죠.

울먹이던 소녀는 거북이들이 멀리 가버릴까 해서 얼른 시냇물에서 나왔어요. 그리고 치마 끝자락을 잡고 물을 짜냈죠. 거북이들은 그리 멀리 가지 않았습니다.

After playing for a while, she noticed two turtles crawling peacefully in the distance.

"Let's follow them!"

In her haste to exit the stream, she stumbled over a pebble and tumbled into the water.

"Oops! It's so cold. My dress! Mom has recently bought it for me…"

"Good heavens! Aren't you cold…?"

Twinkle Star gazed at her drenched figure, unsure of how to help.

She was on the verge of tears. Hastily, she climbed from the stream, worried the turtles would vanish. Grasping her dress's hem, she squeezed out the water. Fortunately, the two turtles were still nearby.

서둘러 거북이들을 쫓아간 꼬마는 큰 소리로 인사했어요.

"거북이 아줌마, 안녕하세요!"

"얘들아 안녕."

온화한 거북이가 가던 길을 멈추고 대답했어요. 엄마 거북이와 아기 거북이는 물에 흥건히 젖은 원피스를 입고 있는 꼬마를 봤지요.

"어디로 가고 있나요?"

"우리는 개울 아래 호수로 가고 있단다."

"호수요? 이 근처에 호수가 있어요?"

"여기서 꽤 멀지만 에메랄드빛 호수가 있지. 울창한 나뭇잎 사이로 여러 가지 꽃들이 피어있는 아름다운 곳이야."

Rushing to catch up with them, she called out loudly to get their attention.

"Hi, Mrs. Turtle!"

"Hi, you guys."

Amiable Turtle paused and replied. Both of the turtles looked at her, noticing her completely wet dress.

"Where are you headed, Mrs. Turtle?"

"We're heading downstream towards a lake."

"To a lake? Is there a lake nearby?"

"Yes, it's a bit of a distance from here. There is an emerald lake encircled by numerous vibrant flowers with lush foliages."

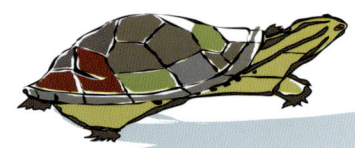

온화한 거북이는 계절에 따라 변화하는 호수 풍경이며, 호수가 가진 신비로움에 대해서도 얘기해주었습니다.

"우와!"

소녀는 호수 얘기를 듣는 것만으로도 감탄했어요.

"그곳은 한참을 가야 해서 힘이 들지만, 너희가 엄청 좋아할 곳이야. 같이 가볼래?"

"좋아요!"

누가 먼저랄 것 없이 소녀와 별은 함께 대답했습니다.

Amiable Turtle informed her of its seasonal changes and the enchantment of the lake.

"Wow!"

She marveled, just hearing.

"It's somewhat remote for us to venture to, requiring some time and effort to reach. Yet it's truly rewarding. Why not accompany us?"

"Sounds wonderful!"

She and Twinkle Star responded in unison.

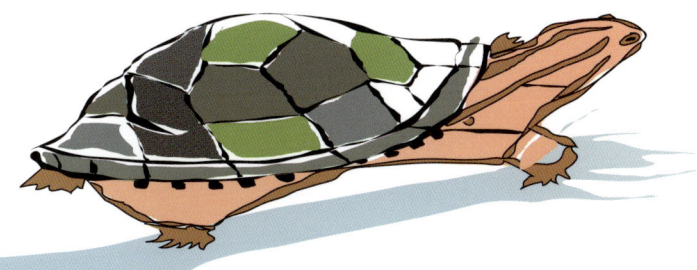

처음에는 주위를 둘러보며 거북이들과 천천히 가는 길이 즐거웠어요. 하지만 소녀의 걸음보다 너무 느린 거북이와 함께 가려면 인내심이 필요했죠. 게다가 큰 개울을 건너면서 아기 거북이를 등에 업은 엄마 거북이가 얼마나 느리던지!
"후유."
그들은 간신히 개울 건너편에 다다랐어요.

Initially, strolling leisurely was pleasant for enjoying the scenery. However, the turtles moved at a much slower pace than she was accustomed to, requiring her to be patient. The situation became more challenging when they reached a large stream. The mother turtle had to carry her offspring on her back. How slowly the mother turtle moved!
"Phew."
Finally, they reached the other side of the stream.

"거북이 아줌마, 좀 더 빨리 걸을 수 없을까요? 우리는 빨리 머물 곳을 찾아야 하거든요."

소녀가 거북이들을 기다리다 지쳐 말했어요. 벌써 뉘엿뉘엿 저물녘이 되었지요. 마음이 급해진 소녀는 거북이들에게 작별 인사를 하고 서둘러 앞서갔습니다.

"Couldn't you walk a little faster, Mrs. Turtle? We'd better hurry to find a place to stay tonight."

She asked worriedly after a long wait. As sunset approached, she could no longer wait for the two turtles. She said goodbye and hurried off.

"어두운 밤길에 너무 서두르지 말아라. 바람은 너의 꿈을 실어 네가 가야 하는 곳으로 불 거야!"

온화한 거북이가 나지막이 말했어요. 거북이들은 꼬마 소녀와 별이 떠난 후에도 한참을 그곳에 서서 바라보고 있었습니다.

"Don't rush it through the night. Let the breeze that carries your dreams guide you to the right place!"

Amiable Turtle softly said. The two turtles remained to watch after they vanished into the distance.

큰 곰이 만들어준 자리
The Night with Big Bear

할머니가 홍차를 따르며 보랏빛 라일락이 활짝 핀 뒤뜰에서 뛰노는 아이들을 봅니다.

"저런!"

돌부리에 걸려 넘어졌다가 툭툭 털고 일어나 다시 힘차게 뛰는 손녀의 모습이 사랑스럽습니다. 그윽한 홍차 향이 할머니를 따뜻이 감싸고, 지그시 눈을 감은 할머니는 지난 여행길을 다시 떠올립니다.

'우린 거북이들에게 작별 인사하고 서둘러 머물 곳을 찾았지. 난 늘 별과 같이 지내고 싶었기 때문에, 저녁에는 별이 하늘에 머무는 것이 낫다고 생각지 못했어...'

As she pours Earl Grey tea into the cup, Grandma watches her grandchildren play in the backyard among fully bloomed purple Lilacs.

"Oh my!"

Seeing her granddaughter trip over a stone, quickly rise, and resume her spirited play, she fondly smiles. Sipping warm tea Grandma reminisces about the journey of her life, half-closing her eyes.

'After saying goodbye to the turtles, we rushed to find a place to stay for the night. As I always wished to remain close to my companion, it slipped my mind that Twinkle Star might be safer in the sky during the night...'

'밤에 시냇가를 따라 걷는 것이 위험해서 우리는 숲길로 들어섰지. 하지만 이미 어두워져 머물 곳을 찾는 게 쉽지 않았어. 그러다 커다란 동굴 입구를 찾았지. 난 안으로 들어가 얼른 잠자리를 찾고 싶었고, 별이 동굴에서 지내는 걸 힘들어했다는 것을 완전히 잊었어. 서두르다 보니 그것을 생각할 만한 여유가 없었지.'

'Fearing a fall into the brook after dark, we headed towards the woods. However, it was too dark to locate a suitable spot. Then, spotting a large cave, I felt an urge to explore it. I overlooked the fact that my friend had previously been unhappy in a deep cave. Being in a hurry, I couldn't make the right decision.'

*   *   *

별은 동굴로 들어가고 싶지 않았지만, 말없이 소녀를 뒤따랐어요. 동굴 안은 아주 어두웠습니다. 꼬마 소녀는 밤을 보낼 만한 곳을 찾았어요. 이곳저곳 둘러보는 동안 무언가 소녀를 향해 갑자기 날아들었어요.

"으악!"

소녀는 깜짝 놀라 몸을 움츠렸습니다.

Initially hesitant, Twinkle Star nonetheless followed her into the cave. It was quite dark inside. Petite Girl hurried to see if there was a place to stay within. As she searched, something abruptly flew at her.

"Yikes!"

She recoiled in astonishment.

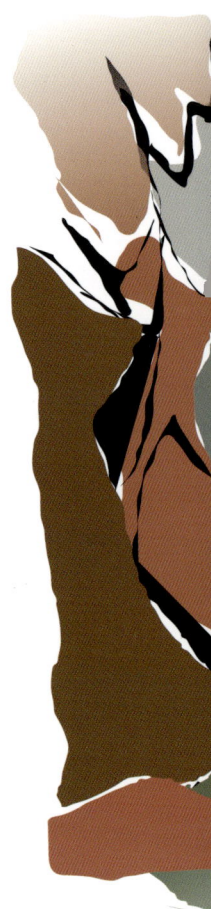

너무 어두워서 무엇이 소녀에게 거의 부딪힐 뻔했는지 알 수 없었습니다. 꼬마는 한 걸음 내딛기도 무서워서 그 자리에 멈칫 섰어요. 바로 그 순간, 별이 반짝이며 소녀가 밖으로 나갈 수 있도록 빛을 비춰주었지요. 꼬마는 별빛을 따라 뛰고 또 뛰었습니다.

It was too dark to discern the flying object that nearly collided with her. She stood paralyzed with fear, finding it hard to move even a step. Just then, Twinkle Star shone brightly, casting his light to guide her way out. She followed the illuminated path, running and running towards the light.

"내게 날아든 건 무엇이었을까?"

"어두운 동굴에 사는 박쥐야. 많이 놀랐지?"

별은 걱정스레 소녀를 보았어요. 소녀는 어디로 갈지 주춤주춤 주변을 살펴보려 했지만, 이미 어둠이 짙게 깔렸습니다. 꼬마는 그대로 주저앉아서 쉬고 싶었지요. 에메랄드빛 호숫가로 가는 길을 알고 있던 거북이들과 함께 가지 않은 것이 후회도 됐습니다. 소녀는 용기를 내서 한 걸음 한 걸음 조심스레 걸었습니다. 소녀의 발걸음을 따라 별은 다시 앞길을 밝게 비추기 시작했어요.

주위에는 짙은 꽃향내가 났습니다. 소녀는 줄줄이 늘어진 꽃을 봤습니다. 밤꽃이었죠. 흰 꽃들은 어두운 밤길을 밝혀주는 듯해서 소녀는 별빛 아래 걷기가 쉬웠어요.

"What were those flying things in the cave?"

"They are bats that dwell in dark places. You seem quite frightened."

Twinkle Star stared at her with a look of concern. She was attempting to find her way, but the darkness made it impossible discern the path. She longed to sit down and rest. She regretted not following Amiable Turtle who knew the route to the emerald lake. Taking courage, she proceeded cautiously, step by step. Once more, Twinkle Star casted his light upon her path.

The air was heavy with the strong scent of blossoms. She observed rows of white flowers dangling; they were Chestnut blossoms. White petals illuminated the path, making it easier for her to walk under the starry night.

한참을 걷다 보니 꽃들 사이로 옅은 회색 물체가 어른거리는 것을 봤어요. 흠칫 놀란 소녀는 급히 별 뒤로 숨었습니다.

"꼬마야, 안녕!"
흐릿한 어른거림 속에서 누군가 친근하게 말을 걸었죠. 소녀는 소리 나는 쪽으로 살금살금 걸어갔습니다. 몇 발짝 가니 큰 곰 한 마리가 있었어요. 꼬마는 무서워서 가까스로 자그맣게 "안녕하세요." 라고 입을 뗐습니다.
"어떻게 여기로 오게 됐니? 너처럼 어린아이에게 이곳은 위험한데..."
"날 따라오면 오늘 밤 지낼만한 곳을 찾아줄게."
칠흑처럼 깜깜한 어두움에서 갈 길을 잃은 소녀는 큰 곰의 친절함이 고마웠습니다.

After walking for some time among the flowers, a large light gray figure loomed, casting a haunting presence. Startled, she swiftly sought refuge behind Twinkle Star.

"Hi, Petite Girl!"
A gentle voice came from afar. She tiptoed towards the source of the voice. After a few paces, she realized it was a giant bear.
"Hi!" she spoke softly, gathering her courage.
"What prompted you to this place? It's quite dangerous for a little girl like you..." "Come with me. I'll take you to a safe place where you can spend the night."
Petite Girl, lost in the pitch-black darkness, was grateful for Big Bear's kindness.

소녀와 별은 밤꽃향이 더 이상 나지 않는 곳까지 곰을 따라 걸었습니다. 한참을 더 가자, 나지막한 평지에 다다랐어요. 큰 곰은 놀라고 지쳐서 쓰러질 듯 걷던 소녀가 걱정됐습니다.
"벌써 밤이 깊었어. 새벽이 올 때까지 내가 여기서 지켜줄 테니, 편히 자라!"

They reached the lower plains where the scent of chestnut blossoms was no longer in the air. Big Bear was worried about her, who seemed to be about to collapse from exhaustion.
"It's quite late. I'll keep watch until dawn. Have a restful sleep, dear!"

큰 곰의 얘기를 듣고 바로 새근새근 잠이 든 소녀를 보고 별은 안심됐습니다. 곰은 소녀가 밤이슬에 옷이 젖지 않도록 커다란 팔을 둘러 소녀를 안아주었습니다.

다음날, 소녀가 일어나 주위를 둘러보니 곰은 어디에도 보이지 않았습니다. 별만이 곁에 있었죠. 소녀는 큰 곰을 다시 볼 수 없는 것이 서운했지만, 찾아볼 여유가 없었습니다. 한시라도 빨리 별과 안전하게 지낼 장소를 찾고 싶었죠. 꼬마는 별과 함께 서둘러 길을 떠났습니다.

Twinkle Star felt reassured, observing she slumbered peacefully next to Big Bear. He embraced her with his big arms to shield her from the chill of the night dew.

The following morning, she awoke to find Big Bear gone. Only Twinkle Star was there. Although she regretted not seeing him again, there was no time to search for him. She had to continue their journey in search of a safe place, hoping to find it soon.

사슴과 만나다
Encounter with Gentle Deer

구름 사이 햇살이 비쳐 초록 나뭇잎이 더 싱그러웠습니다. 꼬마 소녀는 전날 밤 무서웠던 기억을 잊을 만큼 숲의 아름다움에 사로잡혔습니다. 아침 공기가 차가웠지만, 큰 곰의 온기가 남아 소녀를 감싸주었어요. 숲길로 들어선 소녀는 배고픔이 밀려왔죠. 배낭 안에 넣어온 초콜릿과 딸기 웨하스는 거북이들과 걸으면서 다 먹었고, 그 후론 아무것도 먹지 못했어요. 그 때, 멀리 나뭇가지에 달린 작고 붉은 열매들을 봤습니다.

The green leaves of trees, bathed in sunlight filtering through the morning clouds, were revitalized. The forest journey was so wondrous that Petite Girl forgot the previous night's fears. The warmth of Big Bear lingered her until the morning. Hunger pangs struck her as she walked towards the forest. She had consumed all chocolates and strawberry flavored wafers during her walk with the two turtles and hadn't eaten since. At that moment, she caught sight of small red berries nestled among the distant tree branches.

"저쪽으로 가보자."

별은 빨간 산딸기가 있는 작은 동산을 보고 기뻤습니다.

소녀와 별은 한걸음에 나무 아래로 갔어요.

"맛있어 보여!"

얼른 한 알을 따서 입속에 넣은 소녀는 해맑게 웃었습니다. 꼬마는 나무에 낮게 달린 열매를 한 움큼씩 따서 치마 앞자락에 모으기 시작했죠.

"Why don't we go this way?"

Twinkle Star was delighted to discover wild berries on a gentle hillside.

They quickly made their way to the trees where red berries dangled.

"These wild berries look so delicious!"

She picked one and smiled brightly as she tasted it. She gathered the berries one by one from small trees, tucking them into the hem of her skirt.

"와 엄청 달콤해! 너도 먹어봐."

소녀는 얼른 딸기 하나를 집어 별에게 건넸어요. 소녀의 치맛자락에는 산딸기가 어느새 소복이 쌓여갔어요. 꼬마는 먹고 남은 나머지를 호주머니 여기저기에 넣었습니다.

"How sweet they are! Why don't you try some?"

She offered, passing one to Twinkle Star. The lower hem of her skirt brimmed with wild berries. Having quickly eaten some, she crammed the remainder into her pockets.

소녀와 별은 산등성이를 따라 걷고 또 걸었습니다. 꼬마의 치마는 산딸기즙으로 온통 빨갛게 물들어갔습니다. 소녀는 산 위로 가면 안전하게 보낼 곳을 찾을 것만 같았어요. 해가 머리 위에서 쨍하게 비추었습니다. 소녀와 별 주위로 나비들이 팔랑팔랑 날갯짓하며 날았어요. 땀을 뻘뻘 흘리며 등성이를 오르던 소녀는 목이 말랐습니다.

"어디 물이 없을까?"

꼬마는 물을 찾아 주변을 둘러보다가 언뜻 지나가는 것을 봤습니다. 너무 빨리 스쳐 가서 한눈에 무엇인지 알아보지 못했지요.

"방금 지나간 것 봤어?"

소녀가 두리번 거리며 별에게 물었어요.

"깊은 산속에 사는 사슴 같아."

She continued walking until her skirt's hem was completely soaked in red. She believed the upper forest would offer a safe haven. The sun was shining brightly overhead. She and her friend were surrounded by butterflies fluttering about. She felt thirsty as she reached the end of the ridge, perspiring.

"I need some water."

Pausing her climb, she looked for water to satisfy her thirst. Suddenly, she caught a glimpse of something moving swiftly by. It dashed past so quickly that she couldn't identify it at first.

"Did you see the thing that just passed by?"

She asked Twinkle Star, wandering around.

"It could be a deer that resides in the deep forest."

"사슴이라구?" "정말? 아직 주변에 있을지 몰라!"

착한 사람만이 사슴을 볼 수 있다는 얘기가 떠오른 소녀는 이리저리 찾았어요.

몇 해 전, 어느 겨울날, 할아버지는 소녀를 무릎에 앉히고 사슴 얘기를 해주었어요. 사슴의 뿔은 생명을 가진 나무와도 같이, 떨어지고 다시 솟아나기를 반복한다고 했죠. 그리고 사슴들이 사는 높은 산은 오르기만큼이나 내려오기도 힘들다고 말해주었습니다.

"A deer?" "Truly? He might still linger nearby!"

She recalled hearing that only the good-natured could see the deer. She searched for him.

A few years ago, on a winter day, Grandpa sat Petite Girl on his lap and told her a story about a deer. It is said that a deer's antlers are like a living tree, falling and growing again repeatedly. He added that it is equally difficult to descend as it is to ascend the mountain where the deer resides.

꼬마는 덤불을 헤치며 걷고, 무언가 풀숲 밟는 소리를 듣고 우거진 숲을 향해 내달리기도 했어요. 사슴을 찾는 동안 다시 갈증을 느꼈습니다. 하지만 어디에서도 마실 물을 찾을 수 없었죠. 그러다 빛나는 눈망울과 마주쳤어요. 사슴이었죠. 뿔과 털이 나뭇가지와 같은 색이어서 사슴을 알아볼 수 있는 건 반짝이는 두 눈 뿐이었어요.

"꼬마야 안녕!"

상냥한 사슴은 덤불 앞으로 나오길 머뭇머뭇하다, 주변에 해될 것이 없는 것을 알고 소녀에게 다가왔어요.

"이 산등성이는 안전하지 않아. 밤에는 너희를 해칠 수 있는 들짐승이 많이 살고 있어." "내가 산에서 내려가는 길을 알려줄게."

She weaved through the underbrush and circled the untamed forest in search of him, hearing some footsteps. Thirst crept up on her again, yet no water was in sight. Eventually, she spotted a figure with eyes that shimmered like stars. It was a deer. If not for the glint in his eyes, she wouldn't have noticed him since his coat and antlers blending seamlessly with the foliage.

"Hello, Petite Girl!"

Gentle Deer paused, wary, but after ensuring the absence of danger, he stepped into her.

"This ridge isn't safe, especially at night. There are many wild animals that could be dangerous for you." "I'll lead you down to the lower land."

"나를 따라와!"

경중경중 제자리를 맴돌면서 상냥한 사슴은 머뭇거리는 꼬마를 지켜보았어요. 그러고 나서 소녀가 준비되었다고 느낀 사슴은 달리기 시작했죠. 꼬마가 잘 따라오는지 가끔 뒤를 돌아보고 또 앞서가면서 산에서 내려갔어요. 매우 빠른 속도로 산기슭을 내려갔기 때문에 소녀는 생각할 겨를도 옆을 돌아볼 틈도 없이 줄곧 뛰었죠. 꼬마는 열심히 사슴을 따라가느라 어느 곳을 지나갔는지 알 수 없었습니다.

소녀와 별이 안전하게 산 아래에 도착한 것을 확인하자, 사슴은 경중 뛰어 말없이 숲속으로 사라졌습니다. 수풀이 바람에 흩날렸습니다. 사슴 따라 쉴 새 없이 뛰었던 소녀는 무척 목이 말랐어요. 정신없이 뛰느라 땀에 흠뻑 젖은 원피스가 가시덤불에 걸려 찢어진 것도 몰랐습니다.

"Follow me!"

Gentle Deer called, hopping in place as he waited for her who was hesitating. Once he saw that she was prepared to follow, he darted off, glancing back periodically to ensure she was keeping up. Gentle Deer's swift pace left her no time to think or observe. Petite Girl was so focused on the chase that she lost track of her surroundings.

As Gentle Deer sensed safety upon reaching the lower lands, he sprinted into the forest and vanished without a word. The bushes swayed in the wind. After her tiring pursuit, she was so thirsty. The chase was so intense that she failed to notice her dress, drenched in sweat, had been snagged and torn by the thorns of the bushes.

지칠 대로 지친 꼬마는 근처에 물을 찾을 기운조차 없어 주저앉았어요. 그리고 아주 깊은 잠에 빠졌습니다.

쓰러져 잠든 소녀를 보고 놀란 별이 해줄 수 있는 일은 아무것도 없었습니다. 간절히 소녀가 깨어나길 바라며 지켜줄 뿐이었죠. 밤이 되고 하늘로 올라간 별은 친구별들과 함께 밤새 소녀를 더욱 환히 비춰주었습니다. 밤이슬이 소녀의 옷자락에 스며 들었습니다.

Drained of energy, she could no longer search for water and fell to the ground. She suddenly fell asleep, overwhelmed by fatigue.

Twinkle Star was filled with fright and concern, witnessing her sudden slumber. Yet, all he could do was stand vigil, hoping for her awakening. As night fell, he ascended to the sky, casting a brighter glow upon her, joined by the luminous company of his stellar companions. Night dew settled on Petite Girl's dress.

멋진 여우의 집에서
At Charming Fox's House

사슴이 데려다준 곳은 며칠 전 온화한 거북이가 알려준 에메랄드빛 호숫가였습니다. 우거진 초록 나무 사이로 들꽃들이 정겨웠습니다. 아침 산들바람이 잠들어 있는 소녀의 얼굴 위로 불어왔습니다. 그리고 그다음 날도 또 그다음 날도 변함없이 산들바람이 꼬마 소녀에게 아침을 알렸습니다.

별은 소녀가 잠들어 있던 사흘 밤낮을 하늘과 땅을 오가며 소녀를 지켜주었습니다. 소녀가 깊이 잠든 지 나흘째 되는 아침, 별은 다시 희미한 빛을 띠고 소녀 곁으로 왔습니다. 그때 여우 한 마리가 소녀에게로 다가갔어요. 여우는 해가 뜬 후에도 별이 땅에서 꼬마를 지키고 있는 것이 놀라웠어요. 여우가 두 손 가득 호숫물을 담아 잠들어 있는 소녀의 입술을 축여주었지요. 다람쥐도 살며시 가서 나뭇잎으로 소녀의 뺨을 쓰다듬었습니다.

They reached the emerald lake mentioned by Amiable Turtle a few days earlier. Lovely wildflowers were scattered among dense greenery of trees. The morning breeze gently touched Petite Girl's face. It constantly signaled her that morning had broken day after day.

Twinkle Star kept watching over her, ascending and descending, as she fell into a deep sleep for three days. On the fourth day after her slumbering, he descended with dimming light and settled beside her once more. Just then, a fox came near, wondering why Twinkle Star stayed by her side on Earth after dawn. Charming Fox scooped up some water to sprinkle on her lips. A squirrel arrived and softly stroked her cheek with a leaf.

새소리가 호수 주변에 맑게 퍼졌습니다. 소녀는 긴 잠에서 깨어나 자신을 둘러싸고 있는 별과 여우와 다람쥐를 보고 살짝 웃음 지었어요. 별이 곁에 있어서 소녀는 많이 안심됐습니다.

"별아, 내가 얼마나 잔 거야?"

"사흘 낮과 밤. 난 네가 깨어나지 않을까 봐 무척 두려웠어. 괜찮아?"

꼬마는 잠을 자는 동안 밤이면 친구별이 하늘에서 환하게 반짝이며 자신을 내려다본 것이 떠올랐어요. 그 초롱초롱 빛나던 한 무리의 별들이 생각났죠. 하늘에서 내려온 후, 늘 곁에 있던 금빛 별이 밤하늘에 있던 것은 꿈이었을까 생각했어요. 아니면 찬 밤공기에 잠시 깨어 본 것인지도 알 수 없었습니다.

The crystal-clear singing of birds spreaded around her. She awoke with a faint smile to find herself surrounded by Twinkle Star, Charming Fox, and the squirrel. She felt secure with her celestial friend by her side.

"My dear, how long have I been asleep?"

"For three days and nights. I was so worried that you might not awaken. Are you alright?"

She felt as if her friend had been watching over her, twinkling brightly in the night sky as she slept for the last three nights. She recalled the clusters of stars shimmering. She was uncertain whether Twinkle Star's presence in the sky was a dream or reality.

숲에서 지내는 것은 둘 모두에게 안전하지 않았습니다. 소녀가 위험해지면 별이 지켜주느라, 별 또한 위험하게 되지요. 별이 낮에 땅에서 할 수 있는 일은 그리 많지 않았습니다. 밤이 되어 자신의 빛을 비출 때야 소녀에게 도움이 되었죠.

"꼬마야 안녕! 난 산들바람에게서 너희 얘기를 들었단다."
소녀가 깨어난 것이 기뻐서 멋진 여우가 말을 건넸습니다.

The wild forest was unsafe for both herself and Twinkle Star. Should danger arise, he would be at risk too, as he would attempt to protect her. Moreover, there was little for him to do on Earth during the day. Twinkle Star could be helpful when casting his glow upon her in the nighttime.

"Hello, Petite Girl! Sudden Breeze has told me much about you."
Charming Fox said with delight of Petite Girl's awakening.

"여우 아저씨 안녕하세요."

소녀는 허기지고 지쳐서 가까스로 입을 뗐습니다.

"혹시 내가 도와줄 게 있을까?"

"저희가 쉴만한 곳이 있을까요? 며칠을 산속에서 지내서 너무 지쳤거든요."

"이 근처에 내 작은 집이 있단다. 괜찮다면 내 집에서 머물러도 좋아."

꼬마는 여우를 따라 닭 수프 향이 가득한 여우의 집으로 들어갔습니다. 별도 뒤따랐어요.

"Good morning, Mr. Fox."

She replied faintly, weakened by hunger and exhaustion.

"Do you need any help?"

"Could we possibly find a place to rest for a bit? The wild forest has left us exhausted after several days and nights."

"My humble home is nearby. You're welcome to stay if you wish."

She followed Charming Fox into his home, with Twinkle Star trailing behind. The sweet aroma of chicken soup filled the air.

*   *   *

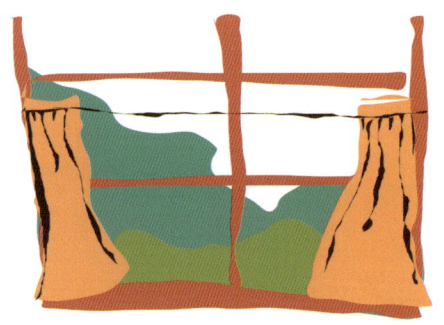

여우는 첫 만남에서 아무것도 먼저 묻지 않았습니다. 김이 모락모락 나는 수프가 소박하게 차려진 식탁으로 안내했지요. 어찌 된 영문인지, 닭 수프는 이미 준비되어 있었던 듯했습니다.

"맛있게 먹어라!"

며칠 만에 먹은 따뜻한 음식은 숲속에서 차가운 이슬 아래 자면서 느꼈던 추위를 녹여주었습니다. 수프를 한 숟갈 또 한 숟갈 다 먹고 나서, 꼬마는 별을 처음 만났을 때부터 호숫가로 올 때까지 모든 일을 여우에게 이야기했죠. 소녀는 열심히 들어주는 여우를 보면서, 늘 귀 기울여 소녀의 얘기를 들어주던 엄마도, 곁에서 껄껄껄 웃으며 듣던 아빠도 생각났어요.

Charming Fox remained silent, leading them to the dining room. They were greeted by tables laden with steaming bowls of soup. The soup appeared to have already been prepared.

"Please, help yourselves!"

The weariness and chill from the night outdoors vanished after consuming the warm food. After she ate the soup, spoonful by spoonful, she began sharing tales of her forest adventures with Twinkle Star. Charming Fox's kind demeanor brought back memories of Mom, who always listened attentively to her stories, and Dad, who would beam with joy at the conversations.

꼬마 소녀는 만난 지 얼마 되지 않았지만, 여우가 오래전부터 알고 지낸 친구처럼 편했습니다. 많은 얘기를 나누지 않았어도 서로를 잘 이해할 수 있었죠. 별도 멋진 여우의 다정함이 좋았습니다.

"근데 넌 왜 별과 늘 같이 있고 싶은 거니? 매일 저녁 서로 만나는 것도 좋을 것 같은데?"
멋진 여우는 소녀가 별과 함께 지내고 싶어서 숲에서 헤매는 것이 걱정되었습니다.
"난 별과 같이 있는 것이 정말 행복하거든요." "힘들어도 별과 함께 지낼 곳을 더 찾아보고 싶어요."

Even though they had met not long ago, it seemed as if they had been acquainted for years. They communicated well with little need for words, understanding each other's thoughts. Twinkle Star could sense the warmth of his friendship.

"Why do you wish to be together constantly? Wouldn't it be simpler to meet each night?"
Charming Fox was concerned about her journey through the forest to be with Twinkle Star.
"Being here with my friend always fills me with happiness." "I know it's difficult, but we might need more time to find the right place."

한참을 뭔가 골똘히 생각하던 여우는 말문을 열었습니다.

"만남에는 새롭게 움터나는 가지들이 있어. 우린 종종 이별을 두려워하지만, 헤어짐이 있어서 때론 또 다른 나뭇가지에서 꽃이 피는 것을 보게 되기도 하지!"

별은 조용히 고개를 끄덕였습니다. 그러나 꼬마는 별과의 이별을 생각조차 하고 싶지 않았어요. 멋진 여우의 이야기가 이해됐지만, 별과 헤어지는 것이 정말 슬펐어요. 소녀는 입을 꾹 다물었습니다.

소녀와 별은 이틀 더 여우의 집에서 보냈어요. 여우 집은 안전했고 만들어 주는 음식은 따뜻하고 맛있었어요. 꼬마 소녀는 멋진 여우에게 고맙고 함께 지내는 것이 편했지만, 별과 함께 여우 집에서 오랫동안 머물 수는 없었습니다.

Charming Fox replied after careful consideration.

"There are new branches sprouting from encounters. We are often afraid of separation, but sometimes it allows us to see flowers blooming on another branch!"

Twinkle Star nodded without a word. She wouldn't think of parting. She grasped Charming Fox's thought, but the burden of saying goodbye was too great for her to bear. She stayed quiet.

She and her friend spent two more days at Charming Fox's home. She found comfort at his house and delight in every meal he crafted. She was grateful for his attentiveness but she sensed that this was not a place where they could remain longer.

여우의 집에서 머문 지 사흘째 되는 날, 꼬마 소녀와 별은 떠나기로 했습니다. 막 여우의 집을 나서려는 소녀에게 여우가 조심스레 얘기했습니다.

"근데 알고 있니? 네가 잠든 사이, 별이 하늘로 올라갔다가 아침이 되면 빛을 잃고 너를 찾아온 것을… 네가 호숫가에서 잠들어 있는 동안 내가 봤어."

소녀는 어리둥절해서 별을 봤어요. 별은 가만히 고개를 끄덕였지요. 꼬마는 자신을 지켜주고 함께 있기 위해, 하늘과 땅을 오가며 힘든 시간을 보냈을 별에게 미안하고 고마웠습니다. 소녀는 별의 손을 꼭 잡고 걸어가며 깊은 생각에 잠겼습니다.

On the third day, she resolved to leave his house. Charming Fox told her, who would soon depart, hesitating to say.

"Are you aware of the secret? Twinkle Star ascended to the sky while you were sleeping and returned at dawn with a softened glow… I witnessed his journey as you slumbered beside the lake."

Puzzled, she gazed at Twinkle Star who nodded silently. She felt a deep remorse for the troubles her friend endured on her behalf. Clutching his hand firmly, she began her walk, immersed in contemplation.

Simply Voyaging 69

돌아가다!
Returning Home!

소녀와 별은 멋진 여우를 만났던 호숫가로 되돌아갔어요. 꼬마는 별과 헤어질 시간이 다가오는 것 같아 슬펐습니다. 호수 주위를 터벅터벅 걷고 또 걸었습니다. 그때, 멀리 호수 위를 나는 한 떼의 백로를 봤어요. 백로의 무리는 무척 아름다워 소녀는 눈을 뗄 수가 없었지요.

Petite Girl and Twinkle Star made their way to the lake where they had first encountered Charming Fox. The sadness that she and her friend might soon part lingered. As she walked on, feeling helpless, a flock of egrets flew high above the lake. The egrets were so captivating that she couldn't look away from them.

"백로들이 어디를 향해 날아갈까?"
말없이 백로를 바라보던 소녀가 별에게 나지막이 물었어요.
"아마도 그들이 왔던 곳으로."
"근데 백로들은 얼마나 멀리까지 날 수 있을까?"
"그들이 가야 하는 곳까지?"
별은 자유롭게 나는 백로처럼 하늘로 돌아가고 싶었습니다. 그러나 혼자 남을 소녀를 걱정스럽게 바라보다가, 다시 백로들에게 눈길을 주었지요.

꼬마 소녀는 갑자기 눈물이 났어요. 별과 헤어짐도 슬펐지만, 두 팔 벌려 안아주던 엄마가 갑자기 보고 싶었습니다. 늘 다투기만 했던 동생도 언니도 보고 싶었죠. 아빠가 "밥 먹자." 불러주던 저녁 시간도 생각났습니다.

"Do you know where the egrets are flying to?"
After a period of silence, she softly asked Twinkle Star.
"Perhaps to where they belong."
"Do you know how far they can fly?"
"As far as they need to?"
He longed to return to the sky as freely as the egrets. Looking at her, he was worried about the friend he would leave behind. The egrets appeared again.

Petite Girl, overwhelmed by tears, deeply regretted the impending separation. Simultaneously, she yearned for Mom's embrace, for the siblings she occasionally quarreled with, and for Dad's voice calling her to a supper.

　그때 백로 한 마리가 호수에 내려앉았습니다. 그 뒤로 한 마리씩 백로들이 내려왔습니다. 그 날갯짓이 얼마나 아름답던지! 꼬마는 한 번도 그렇게 많은 백로의 무리를 본 적이 없었지요.

At that moment, an egret descended onto the lake. Subsequently, several more egrets followed, each descending gracefully in turn. The sight of their flapping wings was breathtaking! She had never before witnessed so many egrets gathered at once.

"한 마리, 두 마리, 세 마리…"

숫자를 세던 소녀가 갑자기 "으앙" 울음을 터뜨렸습니다. 백로들이 춤추며 호숫가로 내려앉는 황홀한 모습에 잠시 눈물을 멈추었습니다. 그리고 말없이 무언가 생각에 잠겼어요.

"별아, 많이 외로웠지?" "너도 백로처럼 하늘에서 자유롭게 지내고 싶을 거야."

"내가 떠나면 너는 괜찮을까?"

별의 목소리에는 슬픔이 묻어났습니다.

"난 너를 잃고 싶진 않지만, 너를 보내주어야 할 때인 것 같아."

별이 하늘로 돌아가야 할 저물녘이 되었습니다. 저녁 기운에 별이 빛나기 시작했지요. 별은 눈물이 그렁그렁한 꼬마를 토닥여주었어요.

"One egret, two egrets, three…"

"Boohoo." Petite Girl who was counting suddenly burst into tears. The sight of their wings, flapping in unison, brought a momentary pause to her sorrow. Silently, she observed them.

"My dear, you have been quite lonely here, haven't you?" "You too would like to be as free as the egrets in the sky."

"Is it okay, if I leave?"

Twinkle Star asked, trembling with sorrow.

"I never wish to lose you, but it's time for you to depart."

Night had descended, and it was time for him to depart. He began to twinkle and gently patted her, whose eyes brimmed with tears.

"내가 늘 그랬던 것처럼 날마다 그곳에 있을게. 내 생각이 나면 눈을 감아봐. 매일 밤하늘에서 별들이 반짝이면, 너는 그 별 중 내가 어디 있는지 알게 될 거야."

터벅터벅 걷는 소녀 뒤로 붉은 노을이 소녀의 얼룩진 원피스를 더 붉게 비추었습니다. 멀리서 엄마가 소녀의 모습을 알아보고 한걸음에 달려왔습니다.
"엄마!"
와락 끌어안은 엄마의 눈에도 소녀의 눈에도 눈물이 흘러 저녁 하늘의 별빛이 비쳐 반짝였습니다.

"I'll be there day and night, just as I have always been. When you need me, close your eyes. Every night, when the stars gleam brightly in the sky, you'll know where I am."

She trudged to make her way home, her blotched red dress standing out against the sunset behind her. From a distance, Mom spotted her daughter returning and hurried out to greet her with open arms.
"Mom!"
Both Mom and Petite Girl's tears glistened, reflecting the light of the stars.

*   *   *

'그렇게 해서 나는 소중한 친구와 작별했지.'

지팡이를 짚고 일어난 할머니는 늦은 오후 햇살에 별 수국의 반짝이는 꽃잎을 그윽하게 바라봅니다. 하늘에 있던 별이 어느새 할머니의 거실에 들어와 한낮에도 반짝였지요. 할머니는 지난날 여행길에서 만난 부엉이와 거북이, 곰과 사슴, 그리고 여우의 눈에도 반짝이던 그 빛이 떠올랐습니다.

할머니가 가만히 가슴에 손을 얹고 미소 짓습니다.

"안녕 반짝이는 내 친구들! 너희는 항상 여기 있어."

그때 열린 거실 창문으로 산들바람이 따사로운 햇살과 함께 후욱 들어왔어요.

"오..." 할머니는 꽃향기를 실은 산들바람을 흠뻑 마십니다.

'That's how I said goodbye to my dearest friend.'

Grandma stands up, steadying herself with her cane. She gazes at Star Hydrangea petals that shimmer like stars, radiating brilliantly in the afternoon sun. Even during the day, a star found its way into the living room's flowerpot. She fondly recalls the journey of the past, the encounters with the owl, the turtles, the bear, the deer, and the fox, all with eyes that twinkled like stars.

She places her hands gently on her chest and whispers with a smile.

"Hello, my twinkling friends! All of you have always been here with me."

Just then, Sudden Breeze wafts through her living room window, accompanied by the warm glow of the sun.

"Ooh..." She inhales deeply, savoring the delightful scent of blossoms brought by the breeze.

닫는 글

나를 찾기 위해 떠난 여행은 글 쓰고 그림 그리는 기쁨의 날들이었습니다. 사랑으로 나를 비춰준 이 세상의 모든 별들에게 이 책을 드립니다. 책 작업하면서 산 넘고 또 다른 산을 넘으며 때론 포기하고 싶을 때, 알 수 없는 힘이 나를 글과 그림 안에 다시 머물게 했습니다. 불어오는 산들바람이 내가 용기있게 나를 바라보고 힘차게 걷도록 인도했습니다.

지금 이 순간 각자의 삶에서 도전하고 분투하는 나의 친구들에게 인사합니다. 이 책이 자신의 길을 찾아가는 당신에게 잠시 멈추어 땀을 식힐 수 있는 휴식처가 되길 바랍니다.

EPILOGUE

Embarking on the journey of self-discovery has been a delightful endeavor, filled with writing and illustrations for this book. I wish to dedicate it to all the "Stars" who illuminated my path. In the process of working on this book, I faced numerous challenges surmounting one mountain after another. When I considered giving up, but each time, an unexpected helping hand appeared, steering me back to my writing and illustrations. A spirit like Sudden Breeze has watched over me, guiding my steps bravely and firmly on new trails.

I hope this book offers a warm "hello" to all "Friends" wrestling with their own challenges "Here and Now." As you read this book, take a moment to pause and refresh yourself along your life's voyage.

꼬마 소녀와 반짝이는 별
PETITE GIRL with TWINKLE STAR

지혜로운 부엉이
WISE OWL

온화한 거북이
AMIABLE TURTLE

큰 곰
BIG BEAR

상냥한 사슴
GENTLE DEER

멋진 여우
CHARMING FOX

아름다운 백로
GRACE EGRET

글·그림 임현아
author • illustrator   Hyunah Lim

작가 임현아는 만남을 소중히 하고 삶에서 잔잔한 행복을 찾는 것을 즐깁니다. 책을 좋아하고 예술을 사랑하며 피아노 치며 기쁨을 느낍니다. 문학과 디자인을 전공했고, 미술 서적을 쓰고 북디자인을 했습니다. 현재 포레드림 출판사를 운영하고 있습니다.

Hyunah Lim cherishes every encounter as a precious gift and finds joy in the simple happiness of life's journey. She relishes moments spent reading books, admiring artworks, and playing the piano. With a background in literature and design, she has authored and designed art books. Presently, she runs her own publishing house, Forêt de Lim.